Jokes for Adults:

(But really only those adults that don't behave like Adults).

By

Bjorn Laffin

My friends laughed when I said that I was writing a joke book.

Well, they're not laughing now.

Two blokes are sitting in a sauna, one keeps staring at the other. Finally the first bloke confronts him.

'What are you staring at?' He asks.

'You're a magician, aren't you?' the other replies.

'Why, yes. I am.' The first man says, actually quite pleased at being recognized.

'Have you been to one of my shows?' He asks innocently.

'Yes, I have.' And then after a short pause. 'And you were terrible, absolutely crap.'

'I beg your pardon?' says the magician somewhat taken aback.

'You could see the rabbit hiding in the hat the flowers sticking out of your sleeve. You were awful, a complete waste of money.'

'I beg to differ, I am an accredited member of the magic circle and have performed all over the world.'

'Look, you were, in my opinion at least, completely useless.'

The magician didn't know how to respond so his accuser decided to give him a chance to defend himself.

'Okay, here we are just the two of us here naked in a sauna, there is nowhere you can hide stuff, so go on show me some magic.'

The magician has a think then replies.

'Right, you stand over there, hands out leaning on the wall facing it, legs apart. As if you were being frisked.'

Looking a bit confused but he did as he was told.

Standing facing the wall as instructed he heard the magician coming up behind him and then suddenly felt something being forced into his asshole.

'Can you feel my thumb up your bottom?' The magician asks.

'I can, I can.' Comes the response, tears in his eyes.

The magician then leans forward and waggles his two thumbs over his complainant's shoulders and either side of his face.

'Now....That's magic !' He says triumphally.

*

What's the difference between men and condoms?

Condoms have evolved, there are not so thick and insensitive anymore.

*

A radio presenter decides to announce a competition during his broadcast. The challenge was to come up with a new word and to put that word into a sentence.

The first few responses were either not really new words or words that couldn't be put into a sensible sentence.

The phone rang one more time.

'Hello caller. Have you got a new word for me?'

'I certainly have.' Was the response.

'Okay, give me your word and I'll check it against a dictionary to see if it already exists or not.'

'Right. My word is Goan... G-O-A-N.'

After a short pause the presenter comes back. 'Well caller I can't find that word in the dictionary so it is indeed a new word. To complete the challenge can you now make a sentence containing your new word?'

'I can, I can.'

'Okay, go for it.'

'My sentence is: Goan fuck yourself.'

The DJ is completely taken aback and slams the phone down on the caller. He immediately apologies to his audience. 'I am so sorry about that, we cannot allow that sort of language on this programme. We will have little music and then we will return to the competition.'

After a few records the presenter is suitably composed to resume the airways. 'I again apologise for that last caller, but we can now resume the competition. Anyone out there how wants to have a go?'

The phone rings almost immediately.

'Hello caller, have you got a new word for me?'

'I do indeed.' Comes the reply.

'And what is this word?' He asks.

'My word is Smee. S-M-E-E.'

After a few minutes research the presenter returns. 'Hello caller, that does indeed seem to be a new word. Now just put into a sentence to win the prize.'

'Okay, here is my sentence: Hello, it's smee again, go and fuck yourself.'

The DJ faints.

*

Why are camels called ships of the desert?

Because they're full of semen.

*

Two blokes are sitting in a bar when one turns to the other and says:

'Hey Donkey boy, it's your round I'll have a pint of Guinness.'

The second guy gets up and duly returns from the bar with a pint of Guinness.'

Just starting to drink, the first chap looks up from his glass and says to the other:

'Hey Donkey Boy, where are the crisps?'

Again, the second bloke got up and did as he was bid.

A little later the first bloke gets up and leaves the table and go to the toilet.

A man sitting at a nearby table and who had heard their conversation, leant over and questioned the one referred to as Donkey Boy.

'Why do you let him speak to you like that?' He asked.

'Awwww Heeeee Aww- always calls me that.

*

I couldn't get my phone to connect to the internet. Then I accidently dropped it into the toilet.

Well, it's syncing now.

*

I have a friend for whom the answer to every question is Alcohol.

He's not an alcoholic. He's just very bad at crossword puzzles.

*

How do two dwarfs greet each other?

'Small world isn't it?'

*

A doctor was giving a lecture to a group of final year medical students. The subject he'd been asked to talk about was 'Involuntary muscle contractions' realising that the subject wasn't particularly interesting and that his audience were quickly becoming bored, he decided to try to liven things up a bit.

He turned to a young lady in the front row and asked her:

'Do you know what your asshole is doing when you have an orgasm?'

'Probably playing golf.' Came the answer.

*

My penis was once in the Guinness book of records.

But the librarian asked me to remove it.

*

Having sex at 75 is still great. It is just more difficult to remember who you're having it with.

*

A doctor was caught in an inappropriate position with a young nurse in his office.

However, he managed to avoid sanctions by explaining that he was actually preforming a life saving manoeuvre.

He had removed his tongue from her throat to stop her from choking.

*

Cliff Richard was giving a concert in Japan but during a pause between songs a member of the audience stood up and shouted:

'Criff, Criff. Sing Itchy sore fanny.'

Cliff Richard decided just to ignore him. But when he had finished the next number, again the man shouted:

'Criff, Criff, Itchy sore fanny .'

Again, Cliff chose to simply ignore him, but when it happened again in the next break, he decided to confront him.

'Look, I'm sorry I really don't sing songs like that.'

The member of the audience looked puzzled. Criff, Criff. Yes, you do, please sing Itchy sore fanny.'

'Look I don't know any such song. Please sit down.'

'You do, you do.' Then he started to sing.

'Itchy sore fanny, how we don't talk anymore.'

*

James Bond is sitting at a bar when an attractive young lady sits down beside him.

He decides to start a conversation with her. So as an opening gambit he turns to her and points to his wrist watch.

She looks a bit puzzled.

But James Bond continues. 'This is a very special watch. Q built it for me. It works on reading telepathic waves coming from someone sitting close and relates important information to me. For example, to let me know if they have a gun concealed on their person and I could be in danger.'

The young woman looks intrigued and asks: 'So what does your watch tell you about me?'

James consults the watch.

'It tells me that you are not wearing any panties.'

'Ahh Ha, it's wrong. I am wearing panties.'

James Bond immediately starts to fiddle with the watch. 'Damn,' he says, 'It must be 20 minutes fast.'

*

I went to the doctor for a prostate examination.

When I asked. 'Where should I put my pants?'

'Next to mine.' Was not the answer I was expecting.

*

What is a blonde's mating call?

'I'm sooooo drunk.'

*

Did you hear about the Irish abortion clinic.

It has a twelve month waiting list.

*

For years I thought my dad suffered from Tourette's. Turns out he just thought I was a fucking cunt.

*

In a recent test for medical students one question asked:

Rearrange the following letters into a part of the body that works best when erect.

PNSIE

The answer was SPINE.

Most of the students failed.

*

My personal trainer said that I had the body of a God.

It's a pity he meant Buddha.

*

Did you know that the secret of success
is sincerity.

- Once you learn to fake that you can
  do anything.

*

My wife asked me what was on the
television.

Apparently 'Dust' wasn't the answer she
wanted.

*

Knock knock.

'Who's there?'

'Alzheimer's.'

'Alzheimer's who?'

nock knock.

*

Why are you holding your face.' One
friend asked the other.

I just got slapped.'

Why? What happened?'

was looking at an old photograph when
a gust of wind blew it out of my hand
and it fell underneath a woman's dress.
So, I asked her. 'Excuse me, can I lift up
your dress, I want to get a photograph.'
That's when she hit me.

*

Fred Astaire and Ginger Rogers were in a
restaurant they had nearly finished their
meal and had just consulted the dessert
menu.

Having made their choices, the waiter went off to fetch them.

On his return and just as he neared the table, he tripped and the desserts flew out of his hands and landed on top of Fred Astaire.

Fred immediately leaped to his feet, looked down at his clothes, now covered in food, and broke into song.

'I've got pudding on my white shirt, I've got pudding on my tails,... '

*

At a school reunion one attendee approaches an old school chum and engages him in conversation.

'You know events like this make me feel like I'm in heaven.'

'Why?' Asks the other. 'Is it because it makes you happy to meet up with old friends?'

'No, no. It's just that I thought that you were dead, he was dead, ...'

*

What do you call a woman with one leg?

- Eileen.

*

What do you call a Japanese woman with one leg?

- Irene.

*

It used to be a taboo subject to talk about what cosmetic surgery a person might have had.

Now you can talk about Botox and nobody raises an eyebrow.

*

When in the gym I have a mantra.

'No pain, no pain.'

*

Why is 'Break a leg.' Said to actors before a show.

- Because every play has to have a cast.

*

I suffer from 'Tom Jones syndrome.'

I can't stop singing *'The green green grass of home.'*

Apparently, *It's not unusual.*

*

What has four legs and flies?

- Two pairs of trousers.

*

I came home from work last night and found a note from my wife stuck to the fridge.

This isn't working. I've gone to stay at my mothers.

I opened the fridge door and the light came on as normal – what is she talking about? It's working fine.

*

I used to be addicted to the Hokey Cokey.

But I turned myself around.

*

Apparently, after the coronation of King Charles, the Government have commissioned a 'Kingmobile' – a heavily armoured car with bullet proof windows, in order to keep him safe.

It is rumoured that the car will cost £450,000.

But actually, that's not to bad, as Prince Andrew's escort cost him £2 million.

*

How did Golf get its name?

When it was invented in the fifteenth century in Scotland it was deemed: **G**entlemen **O**nly, **L**adies **F**orbidden.

*

Answering the door naked is a good way to get rid of Trick or Treaters.

Oh good, here come two more,..
dressed as policemen.

*

A prayer from a Grandson:

Dear God, please send some clothes for
all the poor ladies on Grandpa's
computer.

*

A spider is crawling up the wall of a
kitchen.

The wife asks her husband to kill it.

'I'll catch it in a cup and take it out.' He
says.

He proceeds to put a cup over the spider
then turns the cup over and covers it
with his hand trapping the spider inside.

'Now I'll take it out.' He announces.

'Okay.' Says his wife.

He disappears out the door and doesn't return for some hours. When he does come back, he is clearly drunk.

'Where have you been.' The wife asks.

'We've been to the pub.' He replies.

'Who's we?' She asks.

'Me and the spider. I told you I was going to take him out.'

*

Two men meet in a pub.

'Where are you from?' The first asks.

'Ireland.' Was the reply.

'Ireland, which part?'

'All of me.'

*

Two trees, one a birch and the other a beech tree had grown up beside each other in a forest. Over time a small sapling appeared and started to grow between the two of them.

Both the tall trees watched over and appeared fond of their new smaller neighbour.

One day a woodpecker landed beside the group of trees and so one of the adult trees decided to ask it a favour.

'You are a woodpecker so you know your trees, could you take a sample of our young friend and see if he is the offspring of one of us?

The woodpecker did as he was bid and then returned.

'Well?' asked the two older trees in unison.

The woodpecker looked from one to the other and then replied.

'Nope, he isn't the son of a beech or the son of a birch, but he's the best piece of ash I've tasted in a while.'

*

A poor man dies and goes to heaven. As he enters through the pearly gates he is greeted by Saint Peter.

'You have had a hard and difficult life, but I understand that despite all your own difficulties you were always kind and considerate to others and because of this God and I have granted you a special favour.'

The poor man smiles and asks the nature of the favour.

'Because of your hard life we have granted you a meeting with anyone here in heaven that you would like to meet and chat to.'

'That's fantastic, thank you so much.' The man replies.

'In all of heaven then who would you like to meet?'

The man thinks for a few minutes then answers. 'I think I'd like to meet the Virgin Mary and ask her a question.'

'I'm sure that can be arranged. Leave it with me.' Confirms Saint Peter,

A little while later Saint Peter returns with the Virgin Mary and then leaves them alone to talk.

Shy though he is the man eventually plucks up the courage to speak to the Virgin Mary.

'I am sorry to ask Virgin Mary but in all the paintings and statues I have seen of you, you always look a bit sad and depressed. Can I ask why is that?'

Mary glances about as if to be sure nobody else is listening and then lowers her voice and whispers in his ear.

'I always wanted a girl.'

*

What's does Donald Trump's hair and a thong have in common?

They both barely cover the asshole.

*

I once read a book by Shakespeare.

My friend asked me. 'Which one?'

William, of course.'

*

I told my doctor that I had broken my
arm in two places.

He told me to stop going to those
places.

*

Why did the Venus de Milo fall out of
the tree?

Because she had no arms.

*

Knock, knock.

Who's there?

Well, obviously not the Venus de Milo.

*

The government has thought of a new way to bring down the unemployment rate.

It's going to raise the school leaving age to 52.

*

November is a confusing time for dyslexics.

Their Cocks turn black.

*

There are four people, Prince Harry, Donald Trump, the Pope and a ten-year-old schoolboy. on a plane.

All of a sudden, the plane develops engine problems and is clearly about to crash. They discover that although there are four of them there are only three parachutes. Prince Harry lifts one saying, 'I am a prince and am in line for the throne, albeit down the list a bit but clearly. I should live.' With that he jumps from the plane leaving just two chutes behind.

With that Donald Trump leaps up stating 'I am the smartest President that America has ever had so I need to live to stand again for the Presidency.' With that he grabs at another pack and straps it to his back before jumping from the plane.

That leaves just the Pope and the young boy. The pope leans down and hand on the young man's shoulder, says to him. 'I am eighty years of age. I've had a good life but you have your whole life ahead of you, so you my son, take the last remaining parachute.'

The boy looks up at the Pope and says. 'Don't worry Father we are both going to be okay.'

The Pope looks puzzled.

'Father, there are still two parachutes left, America's smartest president just took my schoolbag.'

*

Did you hear about the two heroin addicts that injected themselves with curry powder instead of heroin?

One has a dodgy tikka and the other is in a korma.

*

The fact that jellyfish do not have a brain yet have survived for over 500 million years, gives hope to many people.

*

A little boy returns home from school and his mother asks him how his day went.

'Well,' it was a bit different.' he replies.

'In what way?' his mother asks.

'Today Grandma drove me to school today instead of Grandpa and we didn't see any Idiots, blind bastards or tossers.'

*

There is a new and simplified urine test to detect underlying illness.

Go and have a pee in the garden:

If ants gather around the puddle – Diabetes.

If the urine smells like a barbeque – High cholesterol.

If you pee on your feet – prostate problems.

If you shake it and it causes you pain – osteoarthritis of the wrist.

If you go back in the house with your penis still hanging out – Alzheimer's.

*

Two old guys are playing golf. One slices his shot into the woods and goes off to find his ball.

He finds it lying beside a tree trunk. Sitting on the tree trunk is a frog.

As he bends down to retrieve his ball the frog suddenly says: 'If you kiss me, I will turn into a beautiful young woman and give you all the sex you want for the rest of your life.'

he old guy immediately grabs the frog
nd stuffs it into his golf bag, zipping it
n.

What did you do that for?' Asks his
laying partner.

At my age, I'd rather have a talking
rog.'

*

Men usually look for a woman's heart.
t's just that her breasts get in the way.

*

My wife thought I should take up yoga
o help me relax.

To be honest, I found that at my age
rying to get into some of the yoga
ositions more difficult and stressful
han relaxing.

However, one good thing came out of it I did learn one singer word that instantly induces a state of utter relaxation.

'Namaste.'

(It means the yoga is over).

*

A man is walking down the road when he comes across another lying in the gutter outside a pub. He has a nose bleed and his clothes are disheveled.

As he helps the poor man to his feet it is obvious that he has had a lot to drink and remains unsteady on his feet.

'What is your name?' the first man asks.

'I think I am God.' Replies the other.

'Don't be silly, come, I'll help you get home.'

'No, wait a minute, I'll prove to you that I am God.'

With that he stumbles towards the pub and pushes open the door to go in.

The other man follows him.

The barman turns and sees the drunk coming in.

'Oh, God !' He says. 'You're not back again.'

*

A lecturer is giving a talk to a class of students entitled: *'A philosophy for a better life.'*

He produces a large empty jar and puts it on the desk in front of him.

Then he reaches down beneath the desk for a box of golf balls.

He pours the golf balls from the box until no more can fit in.

'Is this jar full?' He asks the students.

'Yes.' Comes the reply.

The lecturer then reaches down beneath the desk once more and brings out a box of marbles.

He proceeds to pour as many marbles which pour down into the jar fitting into the gaps between the golf balls.

Finally, when no more marbles will fit in, he again asks the audience.

'Is the jar full now?'

Again, 'Yes.' comes the unanimous reply.

He then retrieves a bag of sand from below the desk and pours it into the jar.

The students watch as the sand trickles down between the golf balls and the marbles. He continues until he can fit no more sand in.

'Is the jar full now?'

The audience look less certain now but again they say that they think the jar is indeed full.

Finally, the lecturer produces two bottles of beer. He sets one down on the desk and carefully pours the other into the jar where it froths up but soaks into the mix.

The students look at each other somewhat bemused.

Having completed the experiment, the lecturer turns and address his audience.

'You may well ask what that was all about.'

The students nod in agreement.

'It is in fact a valuable lesson in life. The golf balls represent the big important things in life that you just have to fit in, such as family, job, home etc.'

The students' interest is piqued.

The marbles represent the less important but nevertheless things you would want in your life. For example, hobbies, sport etc.

The sand, 'he continues, 'represents all the other small things in life that you will try and fit in if you can.'

'But what does the beer represent?' Asks one of the students.

'Well, that is the important bit.

here is always room for a beer with a
riend.'

*

/ly wife said we needed a landscape
;ardener.

told her we couldn't.

)ur garden is portrait.

*

t has just been announced that some
\rcheologists have just found ancient
nanual.

t was titled:

'Irish dancing volume 2 – what to do
vith hands and arms.'

*

Varning!

Do NOT join the new Tesco dating service.

My mate did and he ended up with a bag for life.

*

A middle-aged British tourist visits America for the first time. In New York he finds himself in the red-light district and he enters a brothel.

The madam asks him to sit down and she sends over a young lady to entertain him.

They sit and talk, have a drink, frolic a little, giggle a bit as she sits on his lap.

He whispers something in her ear and she gasps and immediately gets up and runs away.

Seeing this the madam decides to send over a more experienced lady to entertain him.

Again, they have a drink, she sits on his knee and they giggle and frolic a bit. He whispers something in her ear. But immediately she too stands up, and screams 'No way.' And storms off.

The madam is again surprised that this ordinary looking man has asked for something so outrageous that two of her girls will have nothing to do with him. She decides the only thing she can do is send over her most experienced girl. This girl has never said no to anything and the madam felt that nothing this chap could ask for would surprise her.

She sits on his knee, they have a drink they frolic and giggle a bit, then he leans forward and whispers something in her ear.

She stands up smacks him across the face and shouts 'No way buddy!' before storming off.

The madam is by now intrigued, she has been in this business for a long time and she has not witnessed three girls turning down a client before.

It is a while since she herself has down any actual bedroom work, but she's sure that she has said yes to everything was or had ever been put to her. So, as she really wants to find out what this man has suggested to make her girls so angry and besides, she'd like to teach her employees a lesson in behaviour.

So, she goes over to him telling him she is the best in the house. They giggle and frolic a bit then she sits down in his lap.

He leans forward and whispers in her ear. 'Can I pay in pounds?'

*

I recently went on a barging holiday.

There were no boats involved I just kept pushing people into canals.

*

What's small, pink and wrinkly and occasionally hangs out grandpa's pyjamas?

- Grandma

*

On an Aer Lingus flight from Dublin to Boston the air hostess came on the intercom.

'There are 200 passengers on board this flight, unfortunately we only have enough meals for 80 people. So, anyone who volunteers to give up their meal to someone who is hungry will get unlimited alcohol throughout the flight.'

Three hours later the same stewardess announced. 'If anybody is still hungry, we still have 80 meals left.'

*

The kids keep laughing at my failing memory.

They'll not be laughing at Christmas when I forget to put the eggs under the bonfire.

*

Some English scientists having dug done some 10 feet into the ground found traces of copper wiring dating back some 200 years. Their conclusion was that their ancestors already had a telephone network at least 150 years ago.

Not to be outdone by the English, in the weeks that followed, an American archaeologist dug down to a depth of 20 feet and shortly afterwards the New York Times reported that American scientists had found traces of 250 year old copper wire and had concluded that their American ancestors obviously had advanced communication networks at least 50 years earlier than the British.

One week later the Irish Times reported that County Kerry man Seamus O'Flaherty a farmer and self- taught archaeologist had dug down to a depth of 30 feet on his farm and found nothing.

The Irish Times reported that Seamus had concluded that 250 years ago whilst the British and Americans were messing about with cable, the Irish had already gone wireless.

*

I've never owned a brewery, but I'm sure I've drunk at least one.

*

Letter in the local paper:

I am disgusted that fireworks are being let off early this year. It's not even Halloween yet.

My poor dog has been cowering under the Christmas tree.

*

Five catholic men and one woman are drinking coffee just off St Peters square in Rome when they start boasting about their offspring.

'My son is a Priest and when he enters a room, they call him 'Father.' Says the first.

Not to be outdone the next catholic man replies. 'My son is a Bishop and people call him 'Your Lordship.'

The third man retorts. 'That's nothing my son is an Archbishop and he is called Your Grace.'

The fourth Catholic gent then says, 'My son is a Cardinal. When he walks into a room people bow their heads and say 'Your Eminence.'

The fifth man says very proudly. 'My son is the Pope. When he walks into a room everyone kneels down and says 'Your Holiness.'

The turn to look at the solitary woman who is quietly sipping her coffee.

The five men gave her a subtle. 'Well...?'

She sits and proudly replies. 'I have a daughter.

Slim,

Tall,

Blonde,

A 38-24- 34 inch body.

Now, when she enters a room, everybody exclaims,

'Oh My God !'

*

A scientist is giving a talk about the paranormal. He asks the audience.

'Who here believes in ghosts?

About half of the audience put up their hands.

'Of those who do believe in ghosts have actually touched or been touched by a ghost?'

Only a handful keep their hands up.

'Okay, of those that believe in ghosts and have touched or been touched by a ghost have had sex with a ghost?'

Only a single hand remains aloft at the back of the room.

Intrigued, the scientist addresses the one man with his hand still up.

'I've given this talk many times and whilst some people do believe in ghost and some even report that they have touched or been touched by a ghost, I've never before had anybody actually say that they had had sex with a ghost. Tell me about it.'

The man at the back of the room looks embarrassed and fidgets back and forth before replying.

Sorry, I couldn't hear you from back here,..... Ghost?... I thought you said oat.'

*

What is 7 inches long, 2 inches wide and makes women go wild?

- A £100 note.

*

A short fairy tale:

Once upon a time a man asked a girl to marry him.

The girl said 'No.'

After that the man lived happily ever after. He rode motor cycles, went fishing, played golf and went to the pub with his friends whenever he wanted.

He drank as much whiskey and beer as he could hold. He had loads of money in the bank and even left the toilet seat up and farted whenever he wanted.

*

One night I dream about wigwams the next about tepees

I went to see my doctor.

He told me I was two tents.

*

My Thai girl friend says that a small penis shouldn't be a problem in a loving relationship.

I still wish that she didn't have one.

*

Ryanair recently reported losses of £760 million.

Presumably, it was just £9.99 before the additional charges kicked in.

*

Al Qaeda – putting the mental into fundamentalism.

*

Police have confirmed that the man who tragically fell from the roof of an 18th floor Nightclub, was definitely not a bouncer.

*

Five out of six scientists have proven that Russian roulette is harmless.

*

'My doctor has put me on some sort of steroids and I've started growing a penis.'

'Anabolic?' I asked.

'No just a penis.'

*

Cowboys would often put a lantern on their saddle at night so they could find the trail when they were far from home.

This was early Saddle Light Navigation.

*

What do you get if you cross a magician with a dog?

- A Labra-cadabra-dor.

*

What is the result of crossing the Atlantic Ocean with the Titanic?

- Halfway.

*

Why do scuba divers fall backwards into the water?

- Because if they fell forwards, they would still be in the boat.

*

Breaking News:

After the recent missile strike on Poland, The French have surrendered.

*

'How's the new girlfriend?'

'She said she wanted to walk me down the aisle.'

'What did you do?'

'I took her to Tesco's.'

*

My friend Bill, a farmer, recently spent £8,500 on a pedigree Black Angus bull in order to breed from him.

He put it in with the cows and it wouldn't even look at them.

Bill was beginning to think he'd been duped into buying the bull. However, he got the Vet to come and look at him.

The Vet said that the bull was basically healthy, but he gave Bill some pills and told him to feed one a day to the bull.

After the first dose the bull Immediately started to service the cows and even broke through a fence to get to some cows in the next field.

Bill said that he didn't know what sort of pills the Vet gave him, but apparently, they taste like peppermint.

*

Viagra:

It won't make you James Bond.

But it will make you Roger Moore.

*

Apparently, the man who invented
predictive text has died.

May he rust in piss.

*

There is a new Indian variant of Covid.

It is called Vindaflu.

We are all to be offered the Punjab.

Several people who have caught have
been seriously ill, my uncle was in a
Korma for a week and he had only just
buried his Naan.

As only three people were allowed to attend the funeral there was a real Argi Bhaji.

*

A husband was complaining to his wife that he had noyone to play golf with.

'What about Robin?' She asked.

'Would you play with someone who cheats on his score and moves his ball when noyone's looking?' He replies.

'I suppose not.' She says.

'Well nor will he,'

*

A man spots a bottle floating in the sea.

He wades out to try to retrieve it as he thinks that there is a message inside.

As he pulls it out of the water there is indeed a message so he struggles to get the cork out to see what the letter says.

After several minutes effort he finally retrieves the piece of paper from inside the bottle and carefully unfolds it.

It reads: 'You have no new messages.'

*

Today's Mathematics problem:

George is 72, his girlfriend is 23.

How much money does George have?

*

The Pope was visiting Glasgow the other day, and he was preforming miracles.

One young man approached him and asked if he could help him with his hearing.

The Pope put both hands on the young man's ears and said 'How's your hearing now?'

The young man looks up at him and says, 'I don't know. It's not till Tuesday.'

*

Driver: 'What am I supposed to do with this speeding ticket?'

Police Officer: 'Keep it. When you collect four of them, you get a bicycle.'

*

Sign outside a Pub:

Wine is now cheaper than petrol.

Drink, Don't Drive!

*

I was worried about my weight so I rang weightwatchers and asked could they send somebody round.

Their reply – 'Yes we have plenty of those.'

*

Erotic Literature for Premature ejaculation:

Chapter 1.

She looked at him.

The end.

*

When I left school, I passed all my exams except Ancient Greek Mythology.

It was my Achilles kneecap.

*

Procrastination is always a good thing.

You always have something to do tomorrow plus you have nothing to do today.

*

A Zoo purchased a new Gorilla, but she was hard to handle.

The Vet was called and he confirmed she was in heat and the only thing that would settle her down would be if she could mate.

Not having a male Gorilla, the Zoo keeper asked a big Irish labourer who was working there at the time if he would have sex with her for £500.

The labourer said that he would think about it and come back to them tomorrow.

he next he returned and he said 'Yes,
ie would'.

But there were three conditions.

1) No kissing.
2) Noyone could ever know.
3) I'll need a few days to get the
£500 together.

*

Paddy was planning to get married and
asked his doctor how he could tell if his
bride was a virgin.

The doctor said, 'You will need three
things. A can of red paint, a can of blue
paint and a shovel.'

Paddy asked. And what do I do with
these, doc?'

The doctor explained. 'Before the
wedding night you paint one of your

testicles red and the other blue. That night when you drop your pants, if she says,

'That's the strangest pair of balls I ever saw.' You hit her with the shovel.'

*

Sign in France near the English Channel.

'Welcome to Calais, twinned with the UK benefits office.'

*

Why are gay guys so well groomed?

Too much time in the closet.

*

The difference between being young and being old is that when you are old you have dry dreams and wet farts

*

The inventor of autocorrect just passed away.

Restaurant in peace.

*

On a plane bound for New York a flight attendant saw a blonde sitting in the First class compartment and knew that she only had an Economy ticket. She requested that that she move back to the Economy section.

The blonde replied. 'I'm blonde and I'm beautiful, I'm going to New York and I'm not moving.'

Not wishing to start an argument in front of the other customers the flight attendant asked the co-pilot to speak to her.

The co-pilot went down to speak to her as requested, again asking her to move out of the First class cabin.

Again, the blonde replied. 'I'm blonde and I'm beautiful and I'm going to New York and I'm not moving.'

The co-pilot returned to the cockpit and reported the problem to the captain.

The captain said. 'No problem, I'm married to a blonde, I know how to handle this.'

The captain made his way back to the First class section and whispered something in the blonde's ear.

She immediately jumped up and made her way back to the Economy cabin saying, 'Why didn't somebody not just say so?'

Surprised by the response that the captain had got the flight attendant and the co-pilot asked what he had said to her to make her move back into economy.

'Simple,' he said, 'I just told her the First class section wasn't going to New York.'

*

My friend Trevor got thrown out of the Pharmacy the other day.

He had asked the lady behind the counter, 'do you take it up the arse or do you swallow?'

Apparently, she went mental,...!

Trevor still has no idea what do with his suppositories.

*

A husband and wife are having a meal in a restaurant.

They are served by a particularly attractive waitress.

'My you are pretty and such a lovely smile.' Compliments the husband.

'Why thank you Sir.' The waitress beams.

His wife is annoyed by the attention he is giving the waitress and says to him. 'Tell her about your erectile dysfunction George.'

The husband looks up at the waitress and says, 'Allow me to introduce my erectile dysfunction,' and pointing at his wife, 'her name is Alice.'

*

28 degrees in Tenerife feels like 28 degrees.

28 degrees in Ibiza feels like 28 degrees.

28 degrees in Benidorm feels like 28 degrees.

28 degrees in the UK feels like you are being sucked into a volcano and Satan himself is pouring hot lava over you.

*

A dung beetle walked into a bar and said, 'Is this stool taken?'

*

Text message:

'See you later, love you xxx'

'Okay, see you later.'

'Honey it would mean a lot to me if you just put some x's at the end of your replies.'

'Ok, love you too Jackie, Alison and Diane,'

*

A three-year-old is examining his testicles while in the bath.

'Mum,' he asks, 'are these my brains?'

'Not yet.' She replies.

*

Did you hear about the agoraphobic homosexual?

He never got out of the closet.

*

Yesterday I bought five litres of Tippex.

Big mistake.

*

Apparently Covid cases are on the increase in China:

After spreading all over the world for the last two years, the virus has decided to work from home.

*

Two men in a pub.

First man. 'My wife hasn't spoken to me in five years.'

Second man. 'Bejesus, a good woman like that is hard to find.'

*

I'm sweating like a Scotsman at a charity fundraiser.

*

Government Announcement:

To help save money in the current economic climate, the Home Office in conjunction with the Immigration Department are going to start to deport old age pensioners instead of asylum seekers. This will lower welfare benefits and NHS costs.

In addition, older people are easier to catch and will not remember how to make their way back home.

*

Have you ever drunk so much that wife's logic actually starts to make sense?

No, neither have I, but I keep trying.

*

A man sits down on a bus beside a blonde. His trousers are bulging as he has a pocket full of golf balls.

The blonde can't help staring quizzically and the bulge.

Noticing her attentions, he says, 'Golf balls.'

'Oh dear,' she replies, 'I bet that hurts more than tennis elbow.'

*

In World War 1 the British would shout 'Hans?' from the safety of their trench.

Hans being a common German name, a Hans would often pop his head up and reply 'Ja.' A British sniper would then shoot him.

It wasn't long before the Germans caught on. They got together and decided to retaliate. They worked out that John was probably the commonest English name.

So, from his trench a German shouted 'John?'

'Is that you Hans?' Replied the British.

'Ja.' The German replied popping his head above the trench once again.

Bang.

*

Spotted recently on the back of a motorcyclists T shirt.

'If you can read this, the wife has fallen off.'

*

Why do male chauvinists cry during sex?

Pepper spray.

*

Do you know the definition of an intellectual?

omeone who listening to the William
ell overture doesn't think of the Lone
anger.

*

f you had to choose between a
vonderful wife and a really nice car.

Vhich would you pick?

etrol? or Diesel?

*

ust because it's International Women's
)ay, doesn't mean that sandwich will
nake itself.

*

tevie Wonder is giving an open-air
oncert in London. He keeps getting
iterrupted by a man shouting out
etween songs.

'Play Jazz Cord. Play Jazz Chord.'

Initially Stevie just ignores him, but the man persists.

'Play Jazz Chord. Play Jazz Chord.'

So eventually Stevie Wonder stops playing and leans down to address the man.

'Look, I don't know what you are talking about, I don't play Jazz.'

Puzzled, the man shouts back, 'Yes, yes, you do.'

Then he starts to sing.

' *I jazz chord to say I love you,...*'

*

I told my wife that I'd changed my mind.

She said 'Good, about time. I hope the new one works better than the last one.

*

'Mmmm,...that smells expensive. What are you wearing?' She asks.

Him. 'Petrol.'

*

When the price of home heating oil starts to soar a useful notice to place in front of your climate control adjuster.

Have you got socks on?

A long sleeve shirt?

Underwear and Pants?

Is your breath invisible?

 If you answered 'Yes' to all of the above – No heat needed.

If you answered 'No' to all of the above – Get dressed.

*

Fuel prices may be rising, but that won't affect me.

I only ever put £20 in.

*

I asked my husband, 'Would you still love me if you won the lottery?'

He replied. 'Of course, I'd still love you. I'd miss you, but I'd still love you.'

*

Seen outside a pub on an English football match day.

'What do you call an Englishman holding a bottle of Champagne after the match?'

'A waiter.'

*

Three Irish men were sitting in a pub. Mick, Pat and Tat. The barman asks. 'Are you guys related?'

Mick says, 'Yes, we're triplets.'

The barman looks puzzled. 'Triplets? But then how come you and Pat are 6ft tall and Tat is only 4ft 6?

'Well, you see,' replies Mick. 'Pat and I were breast fed so there was no tit for Tat.'

*

With all these new cities being created, some poor sod is going to book a city break and end up in Milton Keynes.

*

My girlfriend asked me to name all the women I've slept with.

I probably should have stopped when I got to her.

*

I've been trying to get an appointment to see my doctor for ages. I finally saw him on Wednesday and showed him the rash on my testicles.

He just ignored me and kept pushing his trolley around Sainsbury's.

*

I'm rubbish at French. I can't count beyond seven.

I think I've got a huit allergy.

*

Donald Trump and Joe Biden are each having a shave at the local barbers in Washington.

The barber asks Donald Trump if he would like some aftershave.

Trump replies. 'Certainly not I don't want my wife to smell me and think I've been in a brothel.'

The barber asks Joe Biden the same question.

'Yes, I think I will.' Replies Joe Biden. 'My wife doesn't know what a brothel smells like.'

*

A man tells his doctor, 'I have a strong wish to live forever. Is there anything I can do?'

'Get married.' Says the doctor.

'And will I live forever?'

'No, but you won't want to anymore.'

*

You know you are getting old when your wife says, 'Let's run upstairs and make love,' and you reply, 'sorry, I can't do both.'

*

A man and his girlfriend are having dinner in a restaurant.

He says to her. 'Say something that will make my heart beat faster.'

She replies. 'Your wife is standing behind you.'

*

To the guy who stole my glasses. You better watch out...

I have contacts.

*

Putin is having a meeting in the Kremlin with his war counsel, discussing the war in Ukraine.

When the meeting ends, Sergi Shoigu, minister of Defense makes to leave. As he does so, Putin's secretary overhears him muttering 'Stupid sick bastard.'

The secretary immediately reports the comment to Putin who summons Shoigu back into his office.

Putin then demands. 'Sergi, would you please repeat what you said as you left the room?'

'I said 'Stupid sick bastard.'

'And to whom were you referring? Asks Putin.

'Volodymr Zelensky, of course.' Was the reply.

'Putin then turns to his secretary, 'and to whom did you think he was referring to?'

*

Do you sweat when you are filling your car with petrol and feel sick when trying to pay for it.

If so, you may have Carownervirus.

*

He: 'What kind of films do you like?'

She: 'I like films where I need a box of tissues with me.'

He: 'Me too !'

*

Although Alzheimer's disease is general a bad thing to have, there are a few benefits.

You are always making new friends, you can laugh at old jokes, you are always making new friends, you can hide your own Easter eggs and you are always making new friends.

*

There are three ways to improve your golf game:

Take lessons.

Practice a lot.

Cheat.

*

It was very windy last night; I'm worried about the caravan in our back garden.

We didn't have one yesterday.

*

A woman calls her mother in law on the phone.

'Can you tell me,' she asks, 'who changes the child if it poops itself?'

'It's always the mother, dear.' Replies the mother in law somewhat condescendingly.

'Okay, can you please come over then, your son has got drunk and shit himself.'

*

A man knocks at a door.

When the woman of the house answers it, it is clear that he is a politician canvassing for votes.

'Madam,' he begins, 'I am a politician and an honest man.'

efore he can continue, she replies, 'and

m a prostitute and a virgin.' Before

lamming the door shut in his face.

*

bunch of orphans are being treated to

lunch in a restaurant by the

Orphanage's owner.

When the waiter comes over however,

e says, 'I'm sorry, I can't serve you.'

Why not?' Says the Orphanage owner.

You see, Sir,' the waiter replies, 'this is a

amily restaurant.'

*

he French television station TF1 has

pologised for spelling the Taoiseach's

ame incorrectly when reporting his

ecent Paris visit.

Visite de Mr Mehole Martin.'

*

It is 2024 and the Irish army has decided to invade Northern Ireland. As they cross the border, they hear a Belfast voice shouting at them from over a hill.

'One Royal Irish Ranger is better than ten Republicans.'

The Irish General laughs and sends ten men up the hill to capture it.

There follows some gunfire and then everything goes quiet once again. The same Belfast voice calls out. 'One Royal Irish Ranger is better than a hundred of yours.'

Annoyed, the Irish General sends a hundred men to capture the hill. Once again there is gunfire for a few minutes and then things go silent again.

Suddenly, the same voice calls out. 'One Royal Irish Ranger is better than a thousand of your Republican soldiers.'

Now enraged, the general sends a thousand of his soldiers off to capture the hill. There follows an hour of gunfire, bombs, explosions, screams and death all around.

Finally, one severely injured Republican solider crawls back. The General comes over to him but before he can say anything the soldier say, 'Don't send any more troops, general, it's a trap! There are two of them.

*

I received a phone call from a gorgeous ex-girlfriend this morning. She had called out of the blue just to see if I was still around.

We chatted for ages, losing all track of time, discussing all the wild romantic times that we had had together.

Finally, she asked if I'd be interested in meeting up again to rekindle a little of that 'old magic'.

I was flabbergasted.

'I don't know if I could keep pace with you now,' I said, 'I'm a bit older, greyer and balder than when you last saw me. Also, I'm not sure that I really have the energy I used to have.'

She just laughed and said she was sure I could 'rise to the challenge.'

'Okay,' I said just so long as you don't mind a waistline that is few inches wider these days! Not to mention a total lack of muscle tone,... everything is sagging, my teeth are a bit yellow and I am developing jowls like a Great Dane!'

She giggled and told me to stop being silly.

She teased me saying that tubby, grey haired, older men were cute and usually made great lovers.

'Anyway,' she said, 'I've put on a few pounds myself.'

So, I told her to fuck off.

*

Scotland have been drawn to play Russia in a play off for the next World cup.

The whole world will be without doubt supporting the country that has suffered so much torment and heartache at the hands of an immoral, power crazy and ,

However, I'm sure a few may be supporting Russia too.

*

Dad, can you explain to me what a solar eclipse is?

No sun.

*

A man joins a very exclusive nudist colony.

On his first day there, he takes off his clothes and starts to wander around. A gorgeous blonde walks by and he immediately gets an erection.

The woman notices his erection and comes over to him and says.

'Did you call for me?'

he man replies. 'No, what do you mean?'

he says. 'You must be new here. Let me explain. It's a rule here that if you get an erection, it implies that you called for me.'

miling, she leads him to the side of the wimming pool, lies down on a towel, eagerly pulling him to her and happily ets him have his way with her.

he man continues to explore the olony's facilities. He enters the sauna, s he sits down, he farts.

Within minutes a large, hairy man umbers out of the steam room and pproaches him.

Did you call for me?' Says the hairy man.

'No, what do you mean?' Asks the newcomer.

'You must be new.' Says the hairy man, 'it's a rule here that if you fart, it implies that you called for me.'

With that the large man spins him around, bends him over a bench and has his way with him.

The newcomer staggers back to the colony's office where he is greeted by the smiling, naked receptionist.

'May I help you?' She asks.

'The man yells at her. 'Here's my membership card. You can have it back. Keep the membership fee of £500, I don't care. I am leaving.'

'But Sir,' she replies, 'you've only been here a few hours. You haven't even had a chance to see all of our facilities.'

The man replies. 'I don't care, look lady, I'm 68 years old. I only get an erection once a month but I fart 35 times a day.....'

*

Strangely, since the new healer Clara, who happens to be a young gorgeous buxom brunette, moved into our village, all the women have stopped having headaches.

*

Have just had my covid jab. It was by Astra and Zeneca.

Two gorgeous young nurses.

It didn't hurt a bit.

*

Man to his dog. 'The neighbour tells me he saw you chasing people on bicycle.

The dog looks up at him. 'He's lying, I don't even have a bicycle.'

*

News reporters around the world are shitting themselves as the new Llanfairpwllgyyngylloggerchyrndrobwlla ntysiligogogoch covid variant has been identified in Wales.

*

It has been reported that female aliens are invading are invading earth and kidnapping sexy, good looking men.

You personally are not in any danger.

*

Wife: 'My aerobics instructor told me I've got the chest of a 23-year-old.'

Husband: 'What did he say about your 60-year-old ass?'

Wife: 'We never mentioned you.'

*

I'm no good at push-ups.

Now, piss-ups,.. that's a whole different story.

*

A guy is sitting at a bar looking miserable and simply staring silently at the drink in front of him.

A big burly guy, obviously looking for a fight sits down beside him, grabs the other man's drink and swallows it in one gulp.

The sad guy just starts crying and sobbing uncontrollably.

The big guy relents and says, 'Hey, sorry man. I was just messing around. I'll buy you another one.'

'No, it's not that,' is the reply, 'this is the worst day of my life. I got sacked from my job and when I left the building, I found that my car had been stolen. The police said that I was unlikely to get it back.

When I rang the insurance company, they said I hadn't paid my last premium, so the policy had lapsed.

I took a taxi home and then left my wallet and credit card I tried to run after him, but he just drove away.'

He continued. 'So, I get to my house and I find my wife in bed with my neighbour.

he just yelled at me and told me to get
ut.

o, I left and came down to this bar.

nd just when I was thinking about
utting an end to it all, you show up and
rink my poison.'

*

Vhat do you call a man with a limp?

iam.

*

Vhat you call a man who can't stand?

leil.

*

Vhat is the most terrifying word in a
uclear power plant?

)oops,..

I went to a party dressed as a chicken night. I met a gorgeous girl who was dressed as an egg. We got on very well and one thing led to another.

Before you ask, it was the chicken.

*

My wife said she was leaving me because of my obsession with the Monkees.

– *I didn't believe her, then I saw her face*

*

Nothing rhymes with orange.

Actually, ...Thinking about it,.. No, it doesn't.

*

Did you hear about the constipated accountant. He couldn't budget.

So, he had to work it out with a pencil and paper.

*

I'd love a drink before sex, but don't you think communion wine just seems wrong, Father?

*

My urine always seems to smell like what I've just eaten or drunk.

I think I need to cut down on the Greek white wine.

*

Somebody said that beer contains female hormones.

I can believe it, the more I drink the more I talk rubbish and can't drive.

*

Adam and Eve lived in Paradise, yet their landlord kicked them out. They had two children, one of whom killed the other.

If that's the case, what hope have I in Glasgow?

*

I have a friend who is gay. He spends a lot of time hanging around in bars and picking up random men. He did seem to be having a great old time.

However, I bumped into him last week and he appeared very depressed.

I asked him what was wrong and he said that he had contracted AIDS.

I told him he should be positive for the rest of his life.

*

When I was young, I was poor.

Now after years of hard honest and painstaking work, I am no longer young.

*

Mother to daughter: If a boy touches your breast you must say: 'Don't.'

If he touches your pussy you must say: 'Stop.'

Daughter: And what if he touches both, do I say: 'Don't stop?'

*

What have Alexander the Great and Winnie the Pooh got in common?

Same middle name.

In my experience there are three types of people.

Those that can count and those that can't.

George Washington: 'I cannot tell a lie.'

Donald Trump: 'I cannot tell the truth.'

Boris Johnson: 'I cannot tell the difference.'

A couple were shopping at Christmas. The town centre was packed and the wife suddenly noticed that her husband was no longer with her.

he was quite upset as they had a lot of hopping to do and she worried that he'd got lost so she rang his mobile.

When he answered she asked him where he was.

He replied. 'Do you remember the ewelers we went to when we first got married and you fell in love with a diamond ring that I couldn't really afford at the time, but I said that I would I save up and take you back and buy it for you someday?'

The wife smiled at the memory and a small tear trickled down her cheek. 'Yes, yes, I remember that shop well.'

Well,' he replied, 'I'm in the pub next door.'

*

A skinny little man gets into a lift, he looks up and sees a huge guy standing next to him. The big guy spots the little man staring at him. He looks down and says, '7 feet tall, 350 pounds, 20 inch penis, 3 pounds of testicles, Turner Brown.'

The little guy goes pale and faints.

The big guy kneels down and helps him recover.

In a weak trembling voice, the little chap says, 'What did you say to me?'

The big man replies: 'I saw you looking at me and I thought I'd just give you the answers to your questions before you asked them. I'm 7 feet tall, I weigh 350 pounds, I have a 20 inch penis, my testicles weigh 3 pounds and my name is Turner Brown.'

'Oh, thank God,' exclaims the little man, 'I thought you said 'Turn around.'

*

What does a social media fan weigh?

An Instagram.

*

I saw a one-armed man going into a second-hand shop.

I thought to myself, I don't think they will have what he is looking for.

*

Golf is a five mile walk punctuated by frequent disappointments.

*

They say you should never criticise anyone until you've walked a mile in their shoes.

That way when you do criticise them you will be a mile away and have their shoes.

*

When the war between Russia and Ukraine broke out, the Americans raised their alert level to 'Nuclear threat.'

The Germans raised theirs to 'Get ready to invade.'

The French declared 'Run and hide.'

The Australians said 'No worries.'

The British have now raised their level from 'A bit annoyed' to 'Frankly a bit cross,' a level not reached since the Battle of Agincourt in 1415.

*

If English is the most spoken language in the world.

What is the least spoken?

Sign language.

*

A bear walked into McDonald's and said to the server.

'Why the big pause?' asked the server.

'I'm a bear for goodness sake.'

*

A blonde goes into a shoe shop and asks to try on a pair of shoes.

'How do they feel?' asks the shop assistant.

'They're a bit tight.' Says the blonde.

The shop assistant looks down at the shoes and says, 'Try pulling the tongue out.'

'Nah, theyth sthill feelth a bith tighth.' Says the blonde.

*

Why do they golfer change his socks?

He had a hole in one.

*

My wife says that I'm addicted to collecting old Beatles albums.

I need 'Help.'

*

What do you call a boomerang that doesn't come back?

A stick.

*

What do people win for living to an old age?

trophy.

*

A little old lady rings up her son and complains, 'I got a new jigsaw puzzle, but when I took all the pieces out of the box none of them seem to fit together, it's far too hard for me. Can you come over and help?'

'What's the puzzle of?' He asks.

'The picture on the box is of a big brightly coloured cockerel.'

'Okay, I'll be over shortly.' He replies.

When he gets there, he looks at the table with bits scattered all over it and the box they came in.

'Mum,' he says, 'I think I know what's wrong. This is a box of Corn flakes.'

*

What do the Mafia and a vagina have in common?

One slip of the tongue and you're in deep shit.

*

Two deaf guys go into a bar.

'What do ya wanna drink? Asks one.

'What?' says the other cupping his ear with his hand.

'What do ya wanna drink? Repeats the first.

'Oh, a pint of Guinneth please.'

'Pint of Guinneth, no problem.' He replies as he sets off for the bar.

'Two pinth of Guinneth, please.' He asks the barman.

The barman looks confused. 'Sorry, what did you say?'

'I'm deef,' says the first man pointing to his ears. He repeats the order. 'Two pinth of Guinneth, please.'

'Oh, I'm sorry Sir,' apologies the barman, 'I didn't realise you had a disability. 'Two pints of Guinness, is that the order?'

'Yeth.' Confirms the deaf man.

'Coming right up Sir.'

A few minutes later the barman sets the two pints down in front of the customer.

'There you are two pints of Guinness. That will be six pounds.'

'Sixth poonds? Six poonds?' Says the astonished customer. 'It was only Fife poonds last week!'

'Ah. Yes Sir, but tonight we have some music.'

'Oh,' replies the deaf guy. 'Muuusic, muusic. What type of muusic ith it? Ith it Jazz?'

'No Sir, it's not Jazz.'

'Ith it Blooes?'

'No Sir, it's not Blues.'

'ith it Rock and Roll then?'

'No Sir it's not Rock and Roll.'

'Oh,' he says, 'Oh, it musth be Boooogie Wooogie then.'

'No Sir, it's not Boogie Woogie.'

Frustrated the deaf man asks. 'Well, what ith it then?'

'Tonight,' replies the barman, 'we are having some Country and Western.'

'Oh.' Replies the customer picking up the drinks and heading back to his friend.

 He sets down the two pints of Guinness and says 'Two pints of Guinneth, they were sixth poonds.'

'Sixth poonds? Sixth poonds?' replies his friend. 'They was only fife poonds last week!'

'Yes, but tonight apparently,..' he says,.. 'apparently, there is some muusic.'

'Oh,' replies his friend. 'Muuusic, muusic. What type of muusic ith it? Ith it Jazz?'

'No, it's not Jazz.'

'Ith it Blooes?'

'No, it's not Bloos.'

'ith it Rock and Roll then?'

'No, it's not Rock and Roll.'

'Oh,' he says, 'it musth be Boooogie Wooogie.'

'No, it's not Booogie Wooogie.'

'Well, what ith it then?' asks the friend.

'Tonight apparently,' comes the reply, 'it is some cunt from Preston.'

Printed in Great Britain
by Amazon

14978043R00071